BITTER LEGACY

Stunned by her father's sudden death and the loss of the family estate to handsome and wealthy Brett Usher, Melanie Lord is devastated. Attracted to this lovely girl, Brett offers her a job at his chateau on the Loire which he runs as a hotel. Melanie realises she is falling in love with her benefactor, and although compromised by his scurrilous cousin Simon, Brett finally realises she is blameless . . .

Books by Dorothy Purdy
in the Linford Romance Library:

CONFLICT OF TRUST

DOROTHY PURDY

BITTER LEGACY

Complete and Unabridged

LINFORD
Leicester

First published in Great Britain in 2001

First Linford Edition
published 2004

British Library CIP Data

Purdy, Dorothy
    Bitter legacy.—Large print ed.—
Linford romance library
1. Love stories
2. Large type books
I. Title
823.9′2 [F]

ISBN 1–84395–535–0

Published by
F. A. Thorpe (Publishing)
Anstey, Leicestershire

Set by Words & Graphics Ltd.
Anstey, Leicestershire
Printed and bound in Great Britain by
T. J. International Ltd., Padstow, Cornwall

1

'No, I won't have it,' Melanie exclaimed, her tone vehement. 'It's all a terrible mistake. It has to be!'

She was still trying to get over the trauma of her father's sudden death, and now she was being presented with more bad news.

Driving to the offices of Templeton, Hope and Templeton, Solicitors and Commissioners for Oaths, that fine June morning, there hadn't been a hint of the trouble that lay ahead. Perhaps alarm bells should have rung in her head, but they didn't. She just walked straight into it.

George Templeton coughed nervously. He was used to advising an older, more sedate clientèle, not a volatile, young woman who questioned everything he said.

'I'm sorry, but there's no mistake, my

dear. Don't think for one moment I don't sympathise with you, Melanie,' he hastened to add, 'but you've no choice other than to accept it, I'm afraid. Now please sit down while I try to explain.'

Melanie slumped down in the nearest chair, trying to hide the shock she knew was evident in her face. What he'd just told her was inconceivable. She stared at him, her blue eyes wide with reproach.

'But it can't be right,' she protested. 'When father died, I would inherit as sole heir. You knew that. You're the family solicitor. And now you're saying — '

'That your father sold the estate just before he died, yes.'

George Templeton shifted uneasily in his chair.

'But the sale was conducted without my knowledge, you see. Your father instructed another solicitor to act for him.'

He coughed nervously and referred to his file.

'In the event of your father's death, the purchaser's solicitor was instructed to contact me. No-one else knew anything about it, except the new owner, of course.'

New owner! Melanie drew in a shaky breath. Why had her father sold Squirrels' Chase, and without a word to anyone? She fought for control as she tried to make sense of it all.

'But it doesn't ring true, Mr Templeton, can't you see that? Father and I had such plans for the estate. And now that he's gone, Squirrels' Chase rightly belongs to me. I don't give a hoot what that other solicitor says. There's got to be a loophole somewhere and I want you to find it.'

George Templeton glanced at her apprehensively over the top of his gold-rimmed spectacles.

'I'm afraid that's impossible, Melanie.'

He held up a letter for her to see.

'This has come from a perfectly legitimate law firm, and the solicitor has merely been following instructions. There's no question of misrepresentation or anything like that, I'm afraid. The sale to Mr Usher is perfectly valid.'

He consulted his file.

'He isn't a man to tangle with by all accounts. He's a leading exponent of leisure pursuits — hotels, marinas, that sort of thing.'

'I'm not interested in what he does,' Melanie interrupted. 'It's wrong, all wrong. What can he want with Squirrels' Chase? He can't turn that into a marina!'

'No, Melanie, it's you who's in the wrong. Mr Usher must have had sound reasons for buying the estate. He's a highly-respected entrepreneur, well-accustomed to the exercise of power.'

Melanie eyed the solicitor wryly.

'You seem to know a lot about him. Did his solicitor tell you all this?'

Of course not,' George Templeton replied. 'A solicitor has a duty of confidentiality. He'd never disclose his client's affairs to a third party. No, to be

4

honest, I was curious about the man, so while I was in town I went to the cuttings' office of the Financial Times and got copies of some recent Press releases.'

He held some cuttings up to the light.

'Now, Melanie, just listen for a moment. These will give you some idea of what you're up against.'

Melanie was lost for words as she listened to Mr Templeton read from the cuttings.

'Brett Usher ponders bid for American land deal,' he read out. 'Brett Usher has agreed to acquire Maritine and Marine in a deal worth millions; Usher to take over as Chief Executive of the International Leisure Services Cartel; Brett — '

Melanie jumped out of her chair.

'All right, I'm suitably impressed. But it doesn't explain why father would sell. There's more to this than meets the eye, and I'm going to get to the bottom of it, no matter how long it takes.'

'Well, you won't have long to wait.'

George Templeton glanced at the letter again.

'Mr Usher has asked to meet you, tomorrow at quarter past two to be precise. It seems there are certain matters he wishes to discuss.'

He pushed the letter to one side.

'It's strange he's back in this country so soon. His current interest seems to be a French chateau on the Loire which he runs as a hotel. His solicitor seemed to think he was still there.'

Melanie shrugged and picked up her handbag, ready to leave.

'His chateau, wherever it is, is no concern of mine.'

Quickly she made for the door with George Templeton hot on her heels.

'You're not destitute by any means,' he pointed out, hurrying to keep up with her as she made for her car. 'You still have the paintings, the silver and all your father's antiques.'

He looked anxious as she started up the engine.

'A word of advice, my dear. Don't try to fight him. He'll make a relentless enemy. Try to charm him. Perhaps he might — '

But Melanie drove off, leaving him in mid-sentence.

Charm him? She'd sooner try to charm a boa-constrictor. He was unscrupulous, there was no doubt of that. And tomorrow, when they met, she would know what to expect.

Her thoughts were in turmoil as she drove home. Home — but for how long? She'd expected to hear that her legacy was just a formality. Instead, she somehow had to come to terms with the fact that she had lost the estate.

★ ★ ★

Next morning, her head ached, and as she recalled the events of the previous day, the ache manifested itself into a throbbing pain. She showered and dressed in a smart cream suit. Power-dressing, she thought, might help to give the impression she still had some rights.

She watched later as Brett Usher's dark grey Jaguar purred up the drive. He stopped the car right outside the front door. A symbolic gesture of possession, she thought. How like a man! She was fighting blind panic at the thought of what he might have to say. Surely he couldn't, wouldn't, throw her out. She swallowed hard, took a controlling breath and stepped down into the hall to meet him.

He was in his mid-thirties, she supposed, tall and fair and lethally attractive. He extended his hand.

'Brett Usher,' he said. 'I believe you're expecting me.'

'Er — yes,' she replied stiffly, schooling her features into a polite smile. 'Please, follow me.'

She led the way into the library.

'I'll be as brief as I can, Miss Lord,' he began. 'I presume you already know — '

'That for some unaccountable reason

you've managed to acquire the estate. Yes, I'm fully aware of that.'

He refused to be drawn.

'The sale was a private matter between your father and me, though perfectly legal, of course. I expect your solicitor has explained the situation.'

She heard her own voice, high and tinny, as she replied.

'But you can't want this house. It's a terrible burden on anyone. The heating system's packed up for one thing. There's all kinds of wet and dry rot and — '

'You're wrong,' he replied. 'It's basically sound. I commissioned a full structural survey before the contract was signed.'

Walking over to the window he watched the grey squirrels playing on the lawn.

'This house holds a compelling attraction for me,' he said. 'I saw it and I was enchanted by it. I was determined to buy it no matter what the restoration work might cost.'

He turned away and looked at her.

'I don't know how much you knew of your father's affairs, but financially he was considerably out of his depth. The bank would only consider the estate in its present condition as collateral for a loan. I, on the other hand, could see further than that. Oh, I agree that it's run down and is crying out for repair, but in this particular setting it has considerable potential.'

Potential for what? Not for some leisure centre, surely. The mere thought of it made her blood run cold.

'But if my father had business debts,' she protested, 'surely they could have been satisfied by selling off some of his other assets. You've only to look round this room for instance. The paintings alone would fetch — '

'Miss Lord, I'm afraid you don't understand,' he interrupted quietly, as if addressing a small child. 'Your father was obliged to sell everything he owned. This is my land, my estate. I own the house and everything in it.'

Melanie sat very still.

She was suddenly so frightened, she hardly dared breathe.

'Everything?' she blurted out finally. 'You own everything? No, I don't believe it. My solicitor said — '

His voice cut through her mantle of pain.

'Your solicitor was probably only aware of the land deal,' he said. 'The value of the contents was agreed between specialist valuers and formed part of a separate sale. And whether or not you want to believe it, I assure you those are the facts.'

Melanie felt stifled and for a moment she thought she was going to faint. She tried to stand up but she almost fell, and he quickly moved to reach her, concern shaping his puzzled face.

'I'm sorry,' he said, as she forced herself to sit down again. 'I thought you knew how matters stood.'

He waited for a few moments to give her time to compose herself.

'The way your father handled his

business affairs was most reprehensible,' he went on. 'To this day, I fail to understand how he could — '

'Stop it, please,' Melanie exclaimed. 'I'm sure it wasn't his fault. Perhaps he was owed large sums of money that he couldn't get his debtors to pay. That might explain it.'

'Careful,' Brett Usher replied. 'Blind belief in someone can be dangerous. The plain fact of the matter is, he spent money he didn't have. You couldn't blame his creditors for wanting to sue. Obviously this has come as a great shock to you,' he went on, 'and you can't be expected to come to terms with it all at once. Trouble is, the house has already been programmed for restoration work, and in order to put that into effect, I'll need vacant possession by the end of the month.'

The end of the month! That was a mere week away. What on earth was she going to do? She flexed her shoulders wearily.

'So you're going to take the house,

the contents, everything,' she finally stammered out.

He didn't reply at first, but paced restlessly over to the window and stood there looking out. Then he turned to look at her again.

'Have you had training of any kind?'

'Not what you'd call formal training, no,' she replied, surprised by the sudden question. 'Horses have always been a passion of mine and I used to teach at the local riding school.'

'I see. Without qualifications, finding work isn't going to be easy, and with no experience, it's hardly likely you'd have much success if you try the usual channels. I, on the other hand, may have just the thing for you.'

His eyes took in the porcelain skin, the deep blue eyes and the blond hair combed into a high chignon on top of her head.

'A classic English rose should go down well in France.'

France? What did he mean? Then she remembered that her solicitor had said he owned a chateau there. One of his business ventures, wasn't it? But what had that to do with her?

'Allow me to explain,' he continued. 'One of my companies, Leisuresearch, owns a chateau on the Loire. Are you familiar with that part of the world?'

Melanie shook her head.

'It's an area of great beauty. During the season, the chateau's run by Jacques Dubois, my major domo and an old family friend. But on the administrative side, I'm badly in need of help. I need someone attractive and intelligent, perhaps inexperienced to start with, but willing to learn. A good communicator who could mingle with the guests and not lose her cool. She must welcome responsibility, appreciate a challenge and rise to it when required. Well, Miss Lord, what do you say?'

'Me?' she blurted out, nonplussed.

But what did she have to lose? As of this moment she had nothing — no money, no current employment, nothing but her pride and her wits. He, on the other hand, had it all — incredible looks and sex appeal, more money than he could spend in a lifetime and a level of intelligence that scorched and challenged.

'You're obviously intelligent,' she heard him go on. 'And despite all you've had to face, you've handled yourself well. Your looks are another plus. You'll need to be computer literate, of course, but that can easily be arranged. In a way, you'll be doing me a favour. If you weren't immediately available, you see, I'd have to set up a series of interviews myself, and frankly I just haven't the time.'

Taking some photographs from his wallet, he spread them on the table in front of her.

'It's a typically French chateau as you can see, but it's been purposely furnished in the English style. The contrast makes it more interesting, I think.'

Following his gaze, Melanie saw an

elegant renaissance-style building, characteristic of the region. Its blue slated turrets and round towers were reflected in a large, ornamental lake in front of the main entrance. She could sense the air of peace and tranquillity that emanated from it, and that was what she needed now, desperately.

'You've got three days before we have to leave,' he went on, 'so that will give you plenty of time to pack. Light casual clothes will be best for the day. The Loire gets very hot in June. And for evenings, may I suggest something soft and sensual?'

He looked at her appreciatively.

'Don't ever forget you're a woman. That will impress my guests most of all.'

'But I'm still not sure,' Melanie ventured warily. 'I need more time, time to think. I can't go, just like that.'

'There's nothing to think about,' he replied. 'I'm taking control of the situation from now on. We'll be taking the overnight ferry to Cherbourg. It's a long drive at the other end so I suggest you wear something light and comfortable.'

He walked towards the door, and instinctively she followed him, thinking how easy he had made it all sound. But it was far from easy for her. She'd lost her home. Didn't he realise what it meant to her?

'I'll ring the day after tomorrow with the final arrangements,' he said. 'Meanwhile, there's certain things I need to do.'

He glanced at his watch.

'I must go.'

He didn't say goodbye. He didn't turn around. He walked straight towards the door, opened it and left!

Melanie stood there helplessly, watching him get into the car. Then almost before she realised it, he'd started the engine and driven off down the drive.

2

During the next forty-eight hours Melanie tried to convince herself that she was doing the right thing. She felt as though she'd been forced into an impossible situation when she was defenceless and unable to fight back.

She'd agonised for hours trying to think of a way out, trying to find some loophole so that she wouldn't have to commit herself so soon. But at least if she went to France she'd have a roof over her head, and a job. Those were the things she had to make her priorities now.

It was only when everything was packed and she'd lugged the suitcases down into the hall that she realised what she was letting herself in for. She'd allowed him to coerce her into leaving. It hadn't been the easiest of decisions and if she hadn't been

18

desperate, she'd never have agreed.

She walked from room to room trying to impress every tiny detail on her mind, making her final farewells. All the cosy strands of her life had been utterly shattered, destroyed. She couldn't believe that she'd never return to the house again.

Brett was as good as his word. She jumped when the telephone shrilled, even though she was expecting his call. He was hardly likely to change his mind at the last moment, was he?

'Like I said, I'll be picking you up tomorrow night,' he said briefly. 'Be ready at eight, and make sure you've had something to eat. The ferry's booked and all the necessary arrangements have been made.'

'But what about the house?' she queried. 'I can't just leave everything. Then there's Mrs Harris, my housekeeper. What shall I tell her?'

Melanie's grip on the telephone tightened.

'I don't like it. It's too complicated.

I don't think — '

'No problem,' he replied, refusing to take no for an answer. 'I've already spoken to Mrs Harris and she's been offered a suitable post elsewhere. She'll tell you all about it in the morning. And as for the house, I've appointed a married couple to take over as house-keepers. They're reputable and they've worked for me before. Oh, and when they arrive, you'll make sure they're comfortable, won't you?'

When she didn't reply, he added in a gentler tone, 'That won't be putting you to too much trouble, will it?'

'No.'

'Good. That's settled then. The restoration work is due to start in a few days' time and the place will be filled with workmen, so it makes sense to have someone reliable at the house. Don't worry, they'll cope. They've always coped before and I don't anticipate any problems this time.'

That stopped her dead in her tracks. So he'd done it all before, had he? No wonder he was taking it all in his stride.

'So you see, there's nothing for you to worry about,' he concluded. 'Everything's under control. See you tomorrow.'

He arrived promptly at eight o'clock the following evening, elegant in a pair of sludgy green trousers and matching shirt. His hair was slightly mussed, which made him look even more compellingly attractive.

'All ready?' he enquired, then on seeing the suitcases stacked in the hall, exclaimed, 'My goodness, those should last for long enough!'

He helped her into the car and she sat grim-faced in the passenger seat while he stored the luggage in the boot. As they drove through the gates of Squirrels' Chase, she gazed out of the window, her blue eyes remote now. She'd forced all visible signs of pain back below the surface, hidden them away.

Although he made small talk on the journey to Portsmouth, he refrained from mentioning the estate, merely asking if she was comfortable before switching on the stereo until the docks came into view.

'We could have taken the ferry to Caen,' he said, 'but I've a special reason for going to Cherbourg.'

She asked if he had business dealings there.

'No, nothing to do with business, I'm glad to say. It's simply that I love the place, and I want to enjoy it, too. We'll arrive on market day, and it has to be seen to be believed. The sights and the sounds, I mean. You've just got to let it wash all over you. There won't be enough time for shopping, I'm afraid, and that's a shame, because if you're anything like me, you'd revel in it, I'm sure.'

Once aboard the ferry, Melanie followed Brett up on deck.

'I've reserved a couple of cabins as we're travelling overnight,' he said.

She wondered how he'd managed to arrange that at such short notice. Just shows what influence can do, she thought.

'The crossing takes several hours,' he went on, 'so I suggest you get some sleep. We'll get something to eat in Cherbourg.'

She tried to take his advice, but sleep just wouldn't come. Perhaps some sea air would help, she thought. Going up on deck she stood watching the water, and the events of the past few weeks forced themselves into the forefront of her mind with unrelenting clarity.

What had been the cause of her father's debts? Why hadn't he taken her into his confidence? And why had Brett Usher been so anxious to buy the estate?

Back in her cabin, she managed to drift off into a troubled sleep and when she awoke she realised that soon the ferry would dock.

'I hope you're hungry,' Brett said as they drove away from the terminal. 'We can grab a bit to eat in Cherbourg at one of the cafés I can personally recommend. It's well worth a visit. You just wait and see.'

As they drove along the colourful harbour, he pointed out the ancient streets and alleyways with their attractive stone houses. Chaos was going on all around them. The place was alive with market stalls, loaded with everything she could think of, fruit, vegetables, geese and hens, ducks, shellfish, dairy produce and brilliant flowers.

Brett laughed as he watched her take it all in.

'It's always like this on a Saturday,' he explained as they sat on the pavement outside the café in the little square. 'Now what can I order for you?'

'Just croissant and white coffee please.'

She watched him give their order and started to relax, enjoying the colourful atmosphere. She would like to have lingered for a while longer, but she could tell by the way Brett wolfed down his croissant that he was anxious to be on his way.

As they headed south, she noticed how much more relaxed he had become, and involuntarily her spirits soared. He couldn't have been more attentive if he'd tried, handing her the maps, and pointing out places of interest along the way.

'As you may have guessed, I deal mainly in leisure pursuits,' he told her. 'The Chateau de Richelieu is a new venture for me and I am determined to make it a success. There is so much for my guests to do, so much to see. Part of your job will be to prepare a suitable itinerary and offer advice.'

He glanced at the map.

'Here we take the road to Le Mans. You've heard of the famous race track, of course. It lies in the northern part of the Loire and is a big tourist attraction. A party of vintage car rally drivers is actually coming to stay and a visit to the racetrack will be the highlight of their tour. There's no public access to the track itself, of course, but there are several interesting bistros and cafés dotted about the place.'

He turned to look at her and smiled. 'A visit to the Le Mans Museum is something you could consider when preparing an interesting programme.'

Melanie sat there, fascinated by what he was saying.

'Now,' he went on, pointing to the map, 'it's time to concentrate on our route. Look for La Fleche and Samur. Can you see them? It's a straight road after that until we reach Chinon. Then we drive due south and we're there. Do you see?'

Melanie did her best to concentrate her mind on the map. There was a kindness in his tone which was quite disarming, making her warm towards him.

'We're almost there,' he said some time later, as she continued to follow the map. 'It's just a few kilometres from here.'

He slowed down suddenly.

'Now this is the tricky bit. Look for a small, wooden fingerpost pointing the way. We'll miss it if we're not careful.'

'Oh, yes, there it is,' Melanie cried. 'Chateau de Richelieu. I'd have missed it if you hadn't told me where to look.'

They drove alongside fields of corn and bright yellow mustard until they were jostled along a rough, narrow track. Then the road suddenly opened up and the chateau was approached through a traditional avenue of lime trees. They drove along a wide gravel driveway flanked on either side by red, blue and yellow flowers.

As they reached the entrance to the chateau, white doves flew from the turrets, their soft cooing filling the air with vibrant sound, while the splashing fountains and the scent of flowers weaved their own hypnotic spell.

Brett stopped and helped her out of the car.

'Well, what do you think?'

'It's beautiful. The most beautiful place I've ever seen.'

Suddenly the front door burst open and a middle-aged man with grey hair and a beaming smile hurried out to greet them. He was introduced as the major domo, Jacques Dubois. Although the season had only just started, he wore a formal black suit, an immaculate white shirt and a grey waistcoat which accentuated his portly frame. He flung his arms wide in an extravagant gesture of welcome.

'Good to see you, Monsieur Brett. Although you have been gone only a few days we have all missed you.'

Turning to Melanie, he executed a little bow.

'So this is the young lady you spoke of. She is charmant, très charmant. Be so good as to follow me, mademoiselle. I will show you to your room and make sure that you have everything you need.'

Melanie glanced at Brett who nodded, and she followed Dubois up an imposing, curved, timber ornamental staircase with a balustrade leading to the upper floor. Brett called out to Jacques from the hall below.

'Jacques, my mother, how is she? I didn't like the look of her when I left. I must go to her. Excuse me, please.'

Jacques showed Melanie her room and from her window she could see the lush parkland that stretched for miles. Her room overlooked the east wing of the chateau and had a large double, canopied bed, a writing desk, easy chairs and a bathroom en suite.

Jacques Dubois bowed again.

'I will leave you now, mademoiselle. Your luggage will be brought up soon. Dinner will be served at nine, in the small dining-room.'

He hesitated when he reached the door.

'You must be tired after your journey. I will ask one of the maids to bring you some lemon tea.'

Melanie had just sat down on the bed when she was startled to hear Brett's voice. Without thinking, she headed towards the sound and saw him standing halfway up the stairs, beckoning to Jacques in an agitated way. She noticed how the tension had crept back into his face.

'Jacques,' he called. 'Jacques, come quickly, please. Maman is in great pain. Send for the doctor, quick.'

Melanie sensed his displeasure when he saw her standing there, and when he spoke, there was a distinct edge to his voice.

'You heard? It is no concern of yours, you understand. Tomorrow I shall expect you to report for work, eight o'clock sharp. Dubois will show you where. I trust you haven't forgotten your reason for being here.'

Melanie stepped back, away from the cold blast of anger she could sense in him. It was at his insistence that she had come. Was he already beginning to regret it? He'd never mentioned his mother. It seemed that she, too, lived in the chateau. Brett looked so lost and ill at ease that every instinct she possessed cried out to her to console him. But she knew there was nothing she could do.

Anxious and concerned, she clung tightly to the balustrade as he strode quickly out of sight.

3

Determined not to be late on her first day, Melanie was up and about by six o'clock next morning. Coffee and croissants had been ordered for six thirty, but she was awake long before that, tingling with excitement and anticipation.

The previous evening, Brett hadn't appeared at dinner, and she'd eaten alone on smoked salmon and scrambled eggs before stumbling into her comfortable bed.

This morning, gazing at the view from her bedroom window, the phrase Brett had used about Squirrels' Chase leaped back into her mind.

'I saw it and I was enchanted by it.'

Seeing the lush parkland, the stepped terraces and the outdoor swimming pool here, she wondered why she had harboured reservations about coming to the chateau. She, too, was enchanted by what she saw.

When she walked into his study at exactly eight o'clock, Brett looked calm and relaxed, his fitted trousers and short-sleeved shirt emphasising his lean, tanned body and muscular strength. He motioned to her to sit down in the chair facing him.

'I'm sorry about last night,' he said, taking a sheaf of papers from his desk. 'I acted abruptly and on impulse, but that was no excuse for my rudeness. My mother also sends her apologies,' he went on, shuffling the papers around. 'Under normal circumstances she would have been here to greet you,' he said, his dark eyes serious. 'She suffers from angina, you see. I'm too anxious, I know, but I'm her only son and I'm only around part of the time. Fortunately what we first thought was an attack turned out to be a false alarm.'

Not knowing what to say, Melanie took the papers he handed to her.

'There are so many things for our

guests to do in this magnificent countryside, that I hardly know where to begin,' he said, watching her through narrowed eyes as she skimmed through the printed script. 'It's a paradise here. Artists and naturalists will love it, and part of your job will be to co-ordinate everything that's on offer so you're able to give advice, organise trips and excursions when they're needed, that sort of thing, as well as keeping track of all the bookings, of course.'

Noticing her startled expression, he paused for a moment.

'Don't look so worried, Melanie. Enthusiasm, that's the key. That counts more than anything, because the other things you'll learn as you go along. If in doubt, lean on Dubois,' he went on. 'He's a tower of strength. I've already primed him to look after you.'

Melanie smiled uncertainly.

'According to these schedules,' she said, indicating the papers, 'there's a lot of work to be done. I didn't realise there would be so much to it.'

He looked up suddenly, his eyes capturing hers.

'What I've told you this morning's only the tip of the iceberg,' he said in an earnest tone. 'There are so many things I want to introduce, like seminars on architectural and cultural appreciation, and wine-tasting. That's very popular in this region.'

That got her attention.

'The Loire Valley's famous for its wines, isn't it?' she remarked.

'You're absolutely right,' he replied. 'And I keep an excellent cellar. They call them caves in France. And today's as good a time as any to show it to you. Come.'

He led the way to the wine cellars through the dense parkland, and she walked beside him in the summer sunshine, breathing in the scent of his musky cologne. She couldn't in her wildest dreams have imagined that the day would start so well.

Once inside the cool cellars, she was fazed at first by the darkness as she walked through a forest of large oak barrels, stacked in two tiers, one on top of the other. There were dozens of wine racks with each bottle placed on its side.

'Most of these are local wines,' he told her, 'nothing fancy, like this crisp, white muscadet from Sèvre et Maine. I don't know your taste, but most women find it too dry.'

They walked past all the local wines, and he took her arm and guided her to the far end of the cellar to where a special area was segregated from all the rest. It was completely enclosed, the only entry being by means of a locked door. Brett drew out a bunch of keys and choosing a small, flat gold one, placed it in the lock.

'And these,' he said, once inside and taking a bottle from the rack and handling it lovingly, 'are the priceless wines. Never in a million years would I part with them, though at auction they'd fetch a fortune.'

Replacing the bottle very carefully in

the rack, he went on, 'And because these wines are irreplaceable, they're locked away, as you can see. Only Dubois and I have the key.'

Carefully locking the door behind them, they walked back outside in silence, blinking as they emerged into the bright sunlight.

'As you've seen, there's a lot to be done,' he said. 'The season's already started and the first of the visitors arrive next week. I suggest we go back to the study and I'll give you some idea of what to expect.'

Sitting Melanie down in front of the computer, he brought up on screen a list of reservations for the following month. She sat there, fascinated, as he clicked the mouse and brought up on the screen various computations of arrivals and departures, tariffs and the like.

'I know you're not computer literate,' he said, 'but don't let that worry you. Just imagine trying to keep all this information in a manual system, or even worse, in your head. It would be a mammoth task, not to mention time-consuming.'

'It's fantastic, if you know how to use it,' she said, impressed, 'but I'm scared to death of anything mechanical.'

'Well, you drive a car, don't you?' he replied tersely. 'And it probably took a bit of time to get the hang of that. There's an excellent training school at Chinon and my first thought was to book you on a crash course there. But if you're really worried, I'll have a teacher sent up to the chateau and she can give you one-to-one tuition for, say, a couple of hours a day. That doesn't sound too daunting now, does it?'

He was as good as his word and Melanie amazed herself with her proficiency in a short space of time. She mastered simple things like word processing at first before graduating to the more complicated spread sheets and databases.

The vintage car rally people would be arriving soon, Melanie knew, and she would be expected to organise their visits to Le Mans, a son-et-lumière performance at a neighbouring chateau and the wine tasting which would take place in the grand hall.

Michel, the chef, always chose the menus, and his staff of four carried out his instructions to the letter. Each morning now Melanie would wander into the kitchen to make her own breakfast of freshly-squeezed orange juice, croissant and coffee.

Today, she peered over Michel's shoulder as he hand-wrote the dinner menus, but the words were far too complicated for her high-school French.

'I'm sorry to be a nuisance, Michel, but could you please translate some of these dishes for me?'

Michel laughed. He was a patient man, and was always ready to assist. He gave her details of each item then turned to her, smiling as he saw she had taken notes.

'Delicious, all of them,' he said,

licking his lips. 'Just wait until you try them.'

Down in the cellar, below the front wing of the chateau, Melanie then watched the staff arranging each table, covering the wooden trestles with pink tablecloths, arranging the silver cutlery and pure linen serviettes. Before too long, pink and white candles would glow in the dark, and bottles of local red and white wine would be set at each place, awaiting the diners. Later, the cellar would reverberate with the sound of music and laughter.

Time was flying by, and Melanie decided to check with Brett that everything was on schedule before she went up to change. She was listening to him explain what he wanted her to do, when the door burst open and a tall, dark-haired man entered the room carrying a suitcase in each hand. He stopped short when he saw them and dumped the suitcases on the floor.

Instantly Brett stiffened. His features darkened and when he spoke, his tone had become sharp.

'Simon! What on earth are you doing here?'

The younger man raised one eyebrow quizzically.

'Brett, old man,' he said, as his gaze swept over Melanie, 'things are certainly looking up around here.'

He walked over to where Brett stood and proffered his hand.

'No welcome for your long-lost cousin?'

His skin was quite white, alabaster white, in startling contrast to Brett's warm, even tan, and his eyes were the lightest shade of blue Melanie had ever seen. But despite his good looks there was a certain weakness about his mouth. It was only when the two men stood facing each other that the likeness was apparent — the same height, the same build, the same feeling that each man wished to dominate the other.

Ignoring the outstretched hand, Brett eyed his cousin warily.

'I can't imagine why you've come

here or what makes you think you'd be welcome. In fact I thought I'd made it perfectly clear that you were never to come here again.'

He looked over to where Melanie stood, self-conscious and perplexed, before turning to his cousin again.

'As you'll be leaving soon there's no need for introductions. And now,' he went on, picking up the suitcases and throwing them in the direction of the door, 'take your bags and get out of here!'

4

The bad feeling between the two men snaked like fork lightning across the room. Brett neither expected nor wanted his cousin here, that much was certain. Feeling embarrassed and in the way, Melanie thought it best to leave the room.

'Excuse me,' she said, edging her way towards the door. 'Perhaps it would be better if I left.'

'Yes,' Brett interposed quickly. 'If you don't mind, I think it might be just as well.'

Without giving either man a back-ward glance, Melanie skirted round the suitcases and left the room, closing the door quietly behind her. Once up in her room, she showered and changed into a sapphire blue dress that exactly matched her eyes. Combing her hair into the high chignon that suited her so well, she stepped into a pair of high-heeled sandals and made her way back down to the cellar dining-room.

She'd intended to eat with the guests, but disturbed by Brett's reaction to his cousin's surprise appearance, she found she'd lost her appetite. She glanced over to where Jacques Dubois was standing behind a long trestle table groaning under the weight of bottles of vintage champagne and various wines.

An attractive woman in her late fifties was sitting in a wheel-chair talking to Jacques. Her green taffeta evening gown was cut on classic lines. Her hair, black as a raven's wing, was coiffed in a modern style, her make-up very tastefully applied. Seeing Melanie hesitate, she gestured to her to join her.

'You must be Melanie,' she said, holding out her hand. 'Allow me to introduce myself. I'm Kate Usher, Brett's mother. Come and join me in a glass of champagne.'

Taking the soft, manicured hand, Melanie gazed into the darkest of brown eyes. Brett's eyes, smiling eyes, she thought to herself, the eyes of a friend.

'I'm so sorry, my dear, that I wasn't able to greet you when you arrived at the chateau,' she said with a smile. 'I was having what Brett calls one of my turns. It turned out to be nothing at all, of course, but my son worries so. I have now been kept quiet and rested quite long enough.'

Melanie smiled. Brett's mother was one of the most attractive women she'd ever seen. She must have been a beauty when she was young.

'Did Brett tell you I lived in the chateau?' she asked. 'No, I don't suppose he did. Oh, dear, do I sound like some wicked relative, locked up in the attic?'

Melanie laughed. Brett's mother obviously had no intention of being kept out of things. The older woman indicated the wheel-chair.

'This is the result of a hunting accident several years ago. No chance of walking again without assistance, I'm afraid. But I won't break into tiny pieces, you know. You don't have to tiptoe around me. You see, I'm a social animal, Melanie. I like to know what's going on. Would it be any trouble for you to let me have a copy of the itinerary you're working on? I'm interested to know what group of visitors to expect next. They've all got such different reasons for coming here. Different tastes, and so on.'

Melanie found herself warming towards this elegant woman.

'Of course I will. It's no trouble at all. Brett arranged for me to take a computer course. To be honest, I was terrified at first. I didn't even know how to switch it on. But now I couldn't manage without it. I'm not mechanically minded, you see.'

'With your looks and application to the job, who needs to be mechanically minded?' Kate Usher replied, her approval obvious. 'Brett's told me very little of your past history. But I do know he's very pleased with the way things are working out.'

She paused for a moment and took a sip of champagne.

'And now that we've finally met,' she went on, 'I hope you'll come and visit me when you're not too busy. But don't let me keep you, my dear. As Brett's hostess, I know you've got work to do.'

Melanie felt hot blood rising to her cheeks. Brett's hostess! How much better that sounded than Brett's employee. Somehow it made her feel closer to Brett, though she knew it could never be anything more than a business relationship.

She sighed. It wasn't easy, being with him, working with him, feeling his fingers brush casually against hers. She couldn't help being drawn to him, but he was her employer, she reminded herself sharply, nothing more or less. She must always remember that. She had to. She must.

Brett didn't show up for at least an

hour, but Jacques Dubois made sure that the wine flowed freely and that everyone's glass was charged. The guests seemed relaxed and enjoyed the meal. In fact, the evening was quite a success. Brett smiled at Melanie from across the room, and it was only at around two o'clock in the morning, when everyone had gone to bed, that she realised how tired she felt.

Brett's mother had returned to her suite, and after taking a final look round, Melanie went up to her room, pleased by the results of her efforts, but exhausted.

Next morning she awoke with a headache. Too much wine and excitement, she supposed. Perhaps an early-morning swim might help.

Donning a bikini, the first swimwear she could lay her hands on, she wrapped herself in a towelling robe and went down to the pool. Thrusting through the warm water, she was executing a steady crawl when a frisson of alarm raced through her. Someone was pulling her legs from under her! She struggled, but was clasped around the waist by firm, masculine hands, then brought to the surface with a splash.

When she'd recovered her balance, she was aware of a man standing next to her in the pool, pushing the wet hair out of his eyes. It was the same man who'd burst into Brett's study the previous night — his cousin, Simon.

'Hello,' he said, 'we meet again. Hope I didn't scare you. After last night I bet you thought I'd be a long way away by now. Well, you're wrong you see. Brett's given me a reprieve, for a few days at least.'

He clambered out of the pool, and Melanie followed him, starting to dry herself on one of the big, fluffy white towels by the poolside.

'However did you manage it?' she enquired in a sarcastic tone.

'Let's say I persuaded him,' Simon replied archly. 'Do I take it you're my cousin's latest amour? With so many business commitments I'm amazed he finds the time.'

'I'm Melanie Lord,' she replied, 'and I'm not anyone's amour. I work here, as a matter of fact, helping Brett with the administration. I lost my home back in England and I appreciate Brett giving me this job. I've no qualifications, you see.'

Simon's eyes raked over her slim figure.

'You've qualifications enough for me,' he said, making it obvious what he meant. 'So you're working for Brett, are you? Does he consider himself your benefactor? That's the line he usually takes with those unfortunates who depend on him.'

He grinned.

'Sometimes he sees himself as my benefactor as well. But he's not being very co-operative at the moment,' he said wryly. 'Not co-operative at all.'

Melanie started to wring the water out of her hair.

'It's obvious you've no time for each

other,' she replied. 'Or that's how it appears to me.'

Simon sat down beneath one of the big umbrellas that fringed the pool.

'Trouble is, he has no time for anyone who isn't a big wheel,' he said. 'I could be. That's the stupid part of it. I could be, if only . . . '

He broke off as Brett walked towards them, his face dark and threatening.

'Oh, no!' Simon remarked. 'Here we go again.'

Brett raised his eyebrows just a fraction when he saw them together, and after a terse, 'Good morning,' to Simon, he turned his back on him and ignored him completely. He turned his attention to Melanie, his displeasure in seeing her with Simon showing in his face.

'Come with me, please,' he said tersely. 'I didn't bring you here to waste your time in idle chat.'

He eyed the bikini with distaste.

'Go and change into something more practical, and come to my study.

There's work to be done.'

He strode away, oblivious to the fact that Simon was making a defiant gesture behind his back. Melanie quickly donned her towelling robe and ran up to her room. She changed into a turquoise cotton dress and tied back her long, blonde hair.

Brett was waiting impatiently, and stood up the moment she entered the room.

'So you've managed to tear yourself away from my cousin, I see,' he said, frowning. 'I'd steer clear of him if I were you, unless, of course, you find him attractive.'

Melanie felt her face scald with colour.

'Don't be absurd.'

'You seemed to be enjoying his company,' Brett went on, sitting down at his desk. 'After what you overheard last night, I expect you're wondering why he's still around.'

'It has nothing to do with me,' Melanie said, glancing sideways at Brett and trying to read his expression.

For some reason she felt she owed him an explanation, but what could she say?

'I'd no idea he was in the pool. He certainly wasn't around when I went in,' she replied. 'He caught me off-guard, and as soon as he had a chance, he told me he was staying on for a few days and that's all there was to it. I must say he seemed pleasant enough.'

'Pleasant?' Brett repeated. 'That's hardly the word I'd use. Scurrilous, perhaps, or isn't that a word you understand?'

Anxious to keep this discussion brief she replied, 'I understand. But I only saw him for a few minutes. I can only tell you how he reacted to me.'

Brett laughed shortly.

'He reacted like any other red-blooded male at the sight of an attractive woman, though he's more subtle than most. Goodness knows, he's had plenty of practice. And that bikini of yours was hardly designed to discourage the attentions of the opposite sex now, was it?'

Heat invaded her face even more as she tried to explain.

'I didn't think. It was early, and I grabbed the first thing that came to hand. How was I to know I'd bump into Simon? Surely you don't think I purposely went out to encourage him.'

'No, of course not. Nothing of the kind. Forgive me, I'm out of order. Simon's a sore point as far as I'm concerned.'

He turned to glance at her, then looked away again.

'You see, he's blackmailing me in a sense.'

Melanie stared in amazement. Blackmail? She thought that would be the last thing Brett would tolerate.

'Yes,' he went on. 'Oh, he didn't say it in so many words, but there's no disguising the fact that's what he meant. My mother suffers from angina, as you know. Ideally she needs to be kept quiet, but she insists on being part of things as no doubt you've noticed. Well, for some reason or other, she's always had a soft spot for Simon. Unfortunately he projects a certain vulnerability and the female sex is taken in by it. His loveable rogue act, I call it. Even my own mother is not immune.'

'But . . .'

'He's threatened to go and see her and tell her some hard-luck story. A pack of lies, of course, but I just can't allow that to happen. She's enjoying better health at the moment and I won't have her upset by some fictitious, meandering tale.'

He stiffened with a renewed sense of anger.

'So we came to an agreement. He'll stay away from her if I allow him to stay at the chateau for a few more days while he clinches some sort of deal. I don't like it, but I've no option, I'm afraid.'

Looking at him, Melanie saw a look of resignation on his face.

'Steer clear of him, Melanie, that's

my advice. He'll come to a sticky end one day. He's been in and out of prison several times already. That's why he looked so pale the night he arrived.'

Melanie's brain careered into shock. Prison? Then she realised Brett had changed the subject and was explaining the schedule for the next few days, so she put Simon out of her mind.

'I'm going to be out of the country for a couple of days,' he told her. 'I'll be driving to Cherbourg at dawn, long before you're awake, so I'll leave things in your capable hands.'

He started to leave the room.

'And don't worry about a thing. I'm sure you'll cope.'

'Goodbye,' she replied with a wan smile. 'Have a good trip.'

She'd miss him. She knew that, and after he'd gone she began on the backlog of work. She wanted the time to go quickly until he returned. Although she hadn't been using any physical energy, she'd kept mentally alert, and she felt quite exhausted by the end of the day. After a light supper that Michel had prepared, she made her way wearily up the staircase to her room.

Drowsily she undressed. Then, pulling on a cool cotton chemise, she brushed out her hair, and was just about to cleanse her face when she heard a soft tapping sound on the door. Before she could decide what to do, she heard a voice calling her name.

'Melanie, Melanie, let me in, please.'

For a few moments, she felt transfixed with fear, but some strong compulsion forced her to open the door. To her amazement, Simon was standing outside. Tousled, rumpled and tired, he stumbled into the room.

'Melanie,' he blurted out, 'forgive me, please. I know I've no right to be here. But I've waited to see you all day and I had to be sure you were alone. I need your help, quite desperately. You see, it's a matter of life and death!'

5

Melanie stood and stared at Simon in utter disbelief. Her tiredness disappeared as if by magic.

'Don't be so dramatic, Simon,' she snapped. 'Please get out of here.'

But looking dejected and ill-at-ease, he made no attempt to leave.

'I'm sorry. I know I shouldn't burden you with my problems,' he said, coming farther into the room, 'especially as you hardly know me. But I've nobody else to turn to.'

'Simon! Apart from the fact that you're invading my privacy, do you know what time it is?'

'I know. I know. I've said I'm sorry, haven't I? But I was hoping to see you earlier. Forgive me, but I thought I'd never get a chance to talk to you, and it's been a long day.'

'Yes, well, it's been a long day for me,

too,' she countered. 'This is about Brett, isn't it?'

'My charming cousin? Yes. I suppose he's been on his best behaviour lately. But you mustn't trust him, Melanie. He'll throw me out the minute it suits him and he'll do the same with you.'

'You're wasting your breath, Simon,' Melanie answered crossly, 'because I'm not listening to a word you're saying.'

'But I must talk to you, in private, when he's not around. If he sees the two of us together he'll jump to the wrong conclusion.'

'He's leaving for Cherbourg first thing in the morning,' Melanie interposed quickly. 'Whatever it is can wait until then, surely. Now go, please!'

Much to her relief he left without another word, and she locked the door behind him, worried in case he might return.

'He'll throw me out,' Simon had said, 'the minute it suits him and he'll do the same with you.'

What could he mean by it, she wondered.

Surely as far as she was concerned, Brett wouldn't do anything of the kind. And Simon? What was it he was so anxious to tell her? What had Brett done to make Simon hate him so much? Despite the fact that she wasn't inclined to believe a word Simon said, she needed to judge for herself and restore some balance to her disordered senses.

Force of habit led her to Brett's study the following day, and she worked hard at her computer wishing he'd never gone away. For once she found it hard to concentrate, knowing Simon would come looking for her before too long. In fact she could see him now, hovering outside the door, dressed in swimming trunks with a towel flung over his shoulder.

She worked on for as long as she could, and when she finally decided to take a break, he ran to the door and made straight for her.

'Let's go to the pool. There'll be nobody around at this time,' he said.

Sitting on one of the sun loungers, he started apologising again.

'Sorry about last night, but I'm pretty desperate, you see. Desperate enough to want to make something of myself. Desperate enough to ask you for help.'

Melanie realised what a contrast the cousins were. Brett would never demean himself by asking for help from someone he hardly knew.

'I've nowhere to go, you see. And I'm only allowed to stay here because of Aunt Kate,' Simon said in a bitter tone. 'My dear cousin thinks I might upset her, you see. He's worried she might have an attack if I tell her the truth about her son.'

He poured himself a large glass of iced orange juice from the jug on the poolside table. Perhaps a cold drink might calm him down, Melanie thought. But as soon as he'd quaffed it down, he was off on the same tack.

'I don't know what that swine told

you about me,' he went on. 'A pack of lies, I'll bet. I've been here before asking for help and he's always turned me down. To hear him talk, you'd think I wasn't one of the family. He's already swindled me out of a fortune, and now that I've actually got something on the boil . . .'

Melanie was startled by the sheer anger in his voice, making her realise how embittered he had become. But she still didn't understand why he was telling her all this.

'Simon,' she said in an impatient voice, 'I don't want to hear any more. If it's money you're after, I can't help you. I've no money of my own, and for the time being at least I have to depend on Brett for a job. I really can't see why you're . . .'

'Asking for your help?' he interrupted.

For the first time that morning he managed a faint smile.

'Because I've figured out a scheme that will free me of Brett for ever. But to carry it off, you're going to have to help me.'

'But . . .'

'Now listen. I've got this deal set up with a local winery, low risk, high return. All I need to clinch it is some ready cash.'

He glanced at Melanie covetously.

'Or something I could convert into cash. And that's where you come in.'

Melanie still didn't understand.

'Me?'

Simon barely paused for breath.

'He's shown you his wine cellar, I suppose. Given you the guided tour? He'd have to, wouldn't he? He can't wait to show it off.'

'Yes.'

'Then he'll have shown you his special wines. How could he resist it? I'll make no bones about it, Melanie. That cellar's stocked with some of the finest wines in the world. They're priceless. That's why he locks them away. That's why only he and Dubois have the key.'

'But I still don't see what you're driving at.'

'You will, Melanie, you will. Just be patient for a little while longer.'

She felt a sharp stab of unease. What had Brett's wines to do with her?

'All I need is one bottle of the stuff. One bottle will fetch a king's ransom.'

Simon rubbed his hands together with glee at the thought of it.

'Oh, I've asked him for one, several times. But he's always turned me down. That's why I'm appealing to you. Help me and I'll be rich. You'll get your share, of course. Just think about it — you'll never want for anything, ever again!'

'You're talking in riddles,' Melanie exclaimed. 'I don't see how I could help. And even if I could, I wouldn't want any part of your . . . '

'Ill-gotten gains?' He finished the sentence for her. 'Don't be a fool, Melanie. I'm not asking you to steal the wine. Merely to help me get the key. Now do you understand?'

'No, I don't understand,' Melanie replied, revolted by the idea. 'And even if I did, there's nothing I could do. Brett has the key, you said so yourself. He carries it around on his keyring. I've seen it.'

Simon was not deterred.

'I know that. All I'm asking is that you borrow it for me. Not steal it, just borrow it. It shouldn't be too difficult. Doesn't he live near you?'

'In the chateau, yes, but I've never . . .'

'Seen his apartments? Really, Melanie, that's very difficult to believe.'

Hot blood scalded her cheeks.

'Difficult or not, it happens to be true.'

'Well, if that's what's bothering you, I'll show you where they are.' He grinned. 'As a matter of fact, they're not very far from yours.'

Melanie started to walk away, but Simon sprang off the lounger and soon caught up with her.

'Simon, I want nothing to do with it,'

she said, quickening her stride. 'If you want the key so badly, why don't you ask Jacques?'

'Dubois? Not on your life. He's too canny for that. Unless he got Brett's permission, he'd never part with it. No, wait, I've a better idea. The masked ball on Saturday night. Brett will be back to check all the arrangements, and in the evening, he'll be changing into his evening clothes.'

Melanie stopped in her tracks. What on earth was Simon on about now?

'I suppose so, but that hardly concerns me.'

'Listen and I'll tell you what I'd like you to do. Go up to his suite on some pretext or other, before he changes into evening dress. And before he does, where is he likely to put his personal belongings, his watch, his cuff-links, his keyring for instance?'

'I don't know. On his dresser, I suppose.'

'Right, that's just the way I see it. Now if you steal quietly up the stairs and get into his apartments — the door's always unlocked when he's in there, I've checked. You can get the key while he's in the shower. Five or ten seconds, that's all it would take.'

Melanie took a controlling breath, and when she replied, her voice was irritable and edgy.

'Will you please shut up about it, Simon? I've told you I want no part of it. Now, please, go away and leave me alone.'

The next day was Friday, and Melanie had just twenty-four hours to check the final arrangements for the masked ball the following night. Multi-coloured lanterns and giant flares would light up the grounds, and at midnight there was to be a fireworks display. A trio from Samur had been engaged to provide the music and Michel would get extra help in the kitchen.

There was still much to be done, but Melanie was grateful for that. It meant that, for a short time at least, she'd be able to put the whole matter of Simon right out of her mind. She was surprised to find that even when she'd checked and double checked everything, she still had time to spare, so she decided to take up Brett's mother's invitation to visit her in her apartment.

'Madame Usher has a suite of rooms in the east wing,' Jacques said when Melanie asked him the way. 'There's a seventeenth century dovecote just outside her door. You can't miss it.'

Melanie tapped on the door and waited until she heard a voice call, 'Come in.'

'Melanie, my dear, what a delightful surprise,' Kate Usher exclaimed. 'I'm delighted you've found your way to me at last. Come and sit here next to me,' she said, indicating the settee, 'and I'll pour you some lemon tea.'

The formal sitting-room was furnished in a delicate lime green and a soft pink. All the paintwork, mouldings and ceilings were white, while clear lime green had been used on the walls above the chair rail with a deeper tone for the panel below. These colours provided a marvellous setting for the owner's giltwood-framed paintings of flowers and birds.

Melanie sat down and took one of the white china cups, and Brett's mother poured out the tea from a silver teapot.

'Now,' she said, settling back against the cushions, 'what do you think of the chateau?'

'It's lovely. The most beautiful place I've ever seen.'

'It was built around 1840 in the Renaissance style as you can see, and replaces a manor, but the actual site goes back to the sixteenth century, I'm told.'

She paused for a moment and took a sip of tea.

'Brett hasn't told me much about your background, but I understand how dreadful it must have been for you losing your home. I assure you I deeply sympathise. Still, even though it was tragic at the time, try to look on the positive side if you can.'

Positive side? What positive side, Melanie thought to herself. Losing Squirrels' Chase had been more than she could bear. Whatever did Brett's mother mean?

'You're wondering about that, aren't you?' Kate Usher continued. 'Well, from what Brett told me the house was greatly in need of repair, and the gardens had been allowed to run wild. Oh, not your fault, my dear,' she hastened to add.

Kate Usher was right, of course. No way could Melanie have afforded to restore the house and gardens to their former glory.

'I think I see what you mean,' Melanie replied. 'The house will benefit from a renovation scheme, and at least there will be some satisfaction in that. But the trouble is, even when every-thing's finished, the estate will be owned by a commercial concern, one of Brett's companies, Leisuresearch.'

She could feel hot tears scald her eyes, and she struggled to control them.

'There is never a day goes by when I don't think about it. After all, it was the family home.'

Kate Usher patted her knee.

'And now this is your home, for as long as you want it to be. And although the chateau's completely different from Squirrels' Chase, it's my hope you will find joy and peace here. Are you an only child?'

'Yes. My mother died when I was two, so I hardly remember her. That left my father to bring me up single-handed and we were very close. He tried so hard to make a good life for us, but he got into financial difficulties, and, well, I expect you've guessed the rest.'

Kate Usher sighed.

'Believe me, I, too, know the sorrow of bereavement. My husband died when Brett was just a young man, and he's pushed himself to succeed in life to live up to his father's reputation.'

She stopped speaking and poured

another cup of tea.

'Would you like some biscuits? Some cake perhaps? I can always ring for it.'

'No, I'm fine,' Melanie replied. 'I'm so interested in what you're telling me that I couldn't eat a thing.'

'Well, as long as I'm not neglecting you. What else would you like to know?'

'About Brett?' Melanie asked, putting down her cup. 'I think I can understand what drives him, now that you've told me about his father. When the family solicitor first told me about Brett I thought I would hate him. I imagined him to be some patronising entrepreneur who wouldn't understand what losing my home meant to me. But, on the contrary, he's been thoughtful and kind, giving me a roof over my head and a job.'

'You make him sound like some saint,' Kate Usher said, laughing. 'And he's not, you know. He's got faults like all the rest of us, and no patience at all for anyone who's out to swindle him.'

Like Simon, Melanie thought, but

kept that thought to herself.

'Eventually he'll want to settle down,' Kate Usher went on, 'when all his projects are complete. He'd like a family and a more settled life by the time he reaches forty.'

She gave Melanie a knowing look.

'Before that, in fact, if my instincts are correct. How are your preparations coming along for the ball? I expect you and Jacques have everything under control.'

Melanie smiled.

'Well, I hope so. I want everything to be perfect for when Brett returns. I couldn't bear to see him disappointed.'

Kate Usher looked at her with pride.

'This is an entirely new project for Brett, very ambitious really. And I hope with all my heart that it's a success, for your sake as well as his. You care for my son, don't you, Melanie, dear?'

'I . . .'

'No, don't interrupt. I've watched you together and I've read the signs. Tell me, am I right?'

Melanie blushed to the roots of her hair.

'Yes. I've grown very fond of him,' she blurted out.

'Fond, Melanie? Are you sure you're using the right word? Now don't be embarrassed, my dear. I'm his mother and there's nothing I'd like better than to see him settle down. And without giving too much away, I think I know exactly how he feels about you.'

Melanie could hardly believe it.

'Even if what you say is true, what chance would I have?' she replied. 'Brett has looks and charm, wealth and undoubted social status. How could I compete with all those wealthy women who come to the chateau?'

Kate Usher laughed.

'He's never had the time for any relationships with any of them, my dear. Oh, I'm not denying that many beautiful women have chased him. But as far as I'm aware, he's never been in love, really in love. Now, Melanie, you mustn't underestimate yourself. I happen to know he was attracted to you from the first moment you met. And now that's settled, let's get back to the masked ball. I'd like to see a guest list, if I may.'

Melanie got up from the settee.

'Yes, of course, I'll get one for you. I have time before the guests return from today's trip.'

'No, don't worry about it now. I'll ask Jacques to bring me one. Brett's business associates will be coming, of course, and the proprietors of the other chateaux. Curiosity will bring them here, if nothing else. Have you checked out the guests' credentials by any chance?'

'Well, no,' Melanie replied. 'I didn't think to.'

'I'd be a bit wary if I were you. There's been quite a run on tickets, I'm told. And while we like to think the majority of the guests are genuine, you never can tell. There's bound to be a few gatecrashers at something like this, and we don't want any unpleasantness.

I'd ask Jacques to keep an eye on things if I were you. Oh, dear, what's that?'

She broke off when she heard a gentle tap on the door.

It was none other than Jacques Dubois, to tell Melanie that Michel had finished designing the menus for the ball, and was anxious to get her opinion.

6

Next morning Melanie walked into Brett's study and was soon busy, engrossed at her computer.

She was concentrating so hard that she was unaware that he had entered silently and was watching her at work.

'You've learned fast,' he said, with a nod of approval. 'I like the way your mind works. You're doing a first-class job.'

He smiled, and she felt his nearness as he bent over her to look at what she was doing. Her whole body burned.

'Everything seems under control,' he said reading through the evening's agenda. 'The buffet will be served at nine o'clock, early for this part of the world, but necessary if we are to get through the programme.'

He smiled again.

'I think you and I are wise to have

decided to dress formally rather than in fancy dress. People will be able to spot us more easily that way. Don't you agree?'

'Yes,' she replied, returning his smile. 'Yes, I do.'

'And what do you intend to wear, may I ask?'

'It's a dress I bought in Paris some time ago,' she said. 'It was expensive and I was tempted, but I've never had the right chance to wear it.'

'Until now,' Brett replied. 'I see. Well, whatever you wear you'll look delightful, I'm sure.'

He walked towards the door and then, on impulse, turned back and looked at her.

'I've just had an idea.'

'Yes?'

'Why shouldn't I have a preview? Why should I have to wait with all the others to admire your gown? No, I won't have it. You will dress and then come up to my apartment for a champagne cocktail. How's that? We've both worked hard for this evening and together we shall drink a toast to its success. Yes, I insist.'

'But . . . '

'You don't know where my apartments are.'

It was more a statement of fact than a question.

'That's easily remedied. I'll show you. Come on, now,' he went on, indicating the computer. 'Switch that off. You'll be working all day if I don't put a stop to it.'

He stood next to her until he saw a blank screen.

'You've really become addicted, haven't you? Hard to imagine you were so nervous about it at first. But like I say to all the staff, you never know what you can do until you try.'

All the staff, he'd said. It was a blow to her. Putting it that way, she was being included among the gardeners, the maids, his major domo, Jacques Dubois. Had she been wrong in thinking she was special or was he only interested in her accomplishments? Was he only pleased that she was making the best use of her time, glad that she saw to it that everything was running smoothly at the chateau?

By what right did she expect him to care for her? His mother was wrong. He'd made it clear that she was nothing more to him than an employee, and she couldn't help her eyes misting over as she followed him out on to the sunlit terrace.

'Your apartment isn't near that of your mother then?' she queried, as she followed him past the large lake and into the west wing, where her own apartment was located.

'No. My feeling is that she's entitled to her privacy,' he replied. 'I don't want to hurt her feelings by allowing her to think she's incapable of looking after herself. She's really very competent, you know. But if she lives in a separate wing from me, it gives her more independence. I don't want her to think I'm watching her all the time.'

So he's capable of deep feelings, Melanie thought to herself. But then he was talking about his mother, wasn't he? Her mind was so confused that she tripped and almost fell as he led her up the stone balustrade leading to his apartment, and immediately he stopped and took her arm.

'Are you all right? I'm sorry, I'd forgotten these steps are rather steep.'

'No, really, I'm perfectly all right thanks,' she replied, not daring to admit even to herself that the light pressure of his fingers on her arm had sent ripples of fire running through her.

'It's my fault. I wasn't looking where I was going.'

He stopped outside a door at the top of the staircase.

'This is where I live. Now, are you sure you'll be able to find the way yourself?'

She nodded, and he continued, 'Don't be any later than eight o'clock. Everything will be organised by then and I'll be able to give you the attention you deserve.'

He looked at her so intently from the darkest of brown eyes that she thought her heart would stop.

'It will give me much pleasure to see you in all your finery,' he said. 'I've a treat in store.'

★ ★ ★

Her dress was in jade green chiffon, cut with deceptive simplicity. The top comprised a cross-over bodice that bared her right shoulder, and the skirt, billowing out from her tiny waist, swirled around her as she moved. She'd found evening sandals and bag in exactly the same shade of green. A delicate gold bracelet interspaced with emerald stones, the one piece of good jewellery her mother had left her, sparkled on her wrist and tiny gold earrings gleamed in her ears.

It had taken her much longer to dress than she'd anticipated and she hastily checked the time. Seven forty-five! She soon found her way to Brett's apartment and knocked on the door before pushing gently against it. It was open, and as she touched it, it swung slightly ajar.

She walked straight into a large salon or sitting-room, dominated by a large white divan. The carpets and curtains were the colour of ripe apricots, and various gilt-framed water colours, mostly of the chateau, lined the walls.

Small table lamps, casting an attractive amber glow were placed in strategic positions around the walls, and two crystal flutes and an ice bucket holding a bottle of champagne stood on a low table in front of the divan.

Through the half-open door she saw a fine bedroom with a draped king-size bed and matching bedroom furniture. There wasn't a dresser, but an elegant writing desk upon which Brett had placed his gold watch, his signet ring, and his set of keys! Simon's request flooded into her thoughts.

Her heart missed a beat. It would

have been easy to remove the gold key, although surely Brett would have checked his keyring before he left the room. Say he didn't though? Say he just picked them up without thinking and not realised the gold key to the cellar was missing?

She drew in a sharp breath. How dare Simon ask her to participate in what amounted to theft from the man who had given her a second chance in life? Staring at the bunch of keys, the mere thought of what he had asked her to do made her blood run cold. The bathroom obviously led off from the bedroom, as she could hear the sound of running water. Brett was taking a shower. Then he walked in without warning, his hair still damp, clad only in a short towelling robe.

'Oh, Melanie,' he exclaimed, tightening the belt of his robe. 'Is that the time? I'd no idea you were here. Sit down, won't you? You should have called out to me.'

He stopped a few feet away from her.

'Excuse me, while I change. I shan't keep you waiting long.'

When he came back into the room, she rose automatically to greet him. Darkly handsome in a pair of black evening trousers and a white tuxedo, his tan and the broad set of his shoulders underlined his virility.

An impression of coiled energy sprang from him, some driving impulse that he held in abeyance.

Her senses reeled as in two short strides he reached her side. Taking both her hands in his, he held her at arms' length, his eyes raking over her, frankly admiring.

'Let me look at you. You're beautiful,' he said, and pulling her towards him, he gently kissed the tip of her nose.

Then, lowering his head, he rained a shower of tiny kisses along the curved line of her neck and the pulse-beat at her throat. She stood transfixed as he smoothed a stray tendril of hair that had escaped from the smooth, elegant chignon when he had held her so close.

Oh, I love him, she thought. I love him. I do. Just knowing that she loved him was enough, even if it could never be realised. She could feel, and that was worth everything. Feeling, caring, no matter if it ended in emptiness, because having the capacity to love was so wonderful.

She knew she had never truly loved any man before.

'I think we'll let the champagne chill for a little while longer,' he said as he held her gently away from him. 'No barrage of questions, I notice as to why I've been away? So far, you haven't said a word. Most surprising, I must say.'

When she didn't reply, his gaze swept over her thoughtfully.

'No questions? Or don't you think it's any of your concern?' he said after a few moments.

She stared at him, perplexed.

'I don't know. I suppose I presumed it was business of some kind.'

'It was business, but the kind of

business I'm sure you'll be interested in.'

He touched her arm gently.

'I know how you felt when your father sold the estate, but you said yourself it was in a shocking state of disrepair.'

She sighed.

'I know. But leaving was a terrible wrench all the same. Of course I'm glad that the buildings are to be restored. It broke my heart to see them going completely to rack and ruin. Nothing would please me more than to see the house restored to all its former glory. It's just that . . . '

She broke off, not daring to go on in case she made a fool of herself in front of him.

How would he ever understand her feelings about Squirrels' Chase?

'That it belongs to one of my companies now,' he finished gently. 'Try to look on the positive side. Think how wonderful it will look when it's fully restored. The gardens, too.'

He paused for a moment to gauge her reaction.

'What I'm leading up to is . . . '

'Don't tell me, I can guess. You've been to see it, haven't you?' she said in little more than a whisper.

She wondered what had suddenly made him go to see it now. He'd never mentioned Squirrels' Chase to her since their arrival at the chateau.

'Yes, I have, not only because I represent the company, but because I wanted to set your mind at rest. I wanted to surprise you. It's coming along quite well. There's still a lot of work to be done and it's only in its early stages yet. Now enough about that. I really think it's time we opened the champagne.'

He went over to the ice bucket and she heard the loud pop of a cork.

'Here,' he said, handing her a flute of the pale liquid. 'I rather think a toast is in order, don't you?'

He poured out a glass for himself and sat down on the divan. She sat beside him, waiting to hear what he would say. He smiled and raised his glass.

'To this moment and to the moments yet to come.'

'Moments yet to come?' she queried, as he refilled her glass. 'Not too many of those moments, surely.'

He gave her a puzzled look.

'Why do you say that?' he asked. 'I could hardly bear to part with you now.'

A sharp knock at the door prevented him from continuing, and he put down his glass with an impatient gesture.

'Who the devil can that be?' he said. 'I thought I'd made it clear I didn't want to be disturbed.'

'Excuse me, Monsieur Brett.'

It was Jacques Dubois standing outside the door.

'I'm so sorry. I know what you said, but I thought you should know that the first guests have arrived.'

'Ah, yes, of course. Merci, Jacques,' Brett said. 'Go on ahead and we will come to greet them.'

Finishing his champagne, he walked

into the bedroom, returning a few seconds later with his keyring in his hand.

'I almost forgot these,' he said, pushing the keys into the pocket of his tuxedo, 'and that would never do. Later in the evening we may run out of wine. Come, Melanie, let's join our guests, shall we?'

7

The chateau blazed like a precious jewel in the darkening sky, illuminated by hundreds of multi-coloured lights strung in the trees. Floodlights bathed the ancient walls in an amber glow. Even the outbuildings were lit by flares, placed at strategic positions around the grounds and the splashing fountains were illuminated by a myriad of coloured lights.

'I've been dreaming up ideas to publicise the place,' Brett had told Melanie on her first day. 'And it occurred to me that a masked costume ball could have a lot of appeal. What do you think?'

Melanie had been surprised that he valued her opinion when she had only just arrived.

'Well, yes, it sounds wonderful,' she had replied. 'Will you be giving prizes for the best costumes?'

'Yes. I've already thought of that,' he'd said, interrupting her train of thought. 'I'm glad the same idea occurred to you. It will say on the tickets that prizes will be presented at midnight for the most outrageous and innovative costumes.'

The ball had soon become the talking point of the district and people had vied with each other to get tickets.

Now, as Melanie stood at Brett's side at the bottom of the ornamental staircase waiting to greet the guests, he pointed out the proprietors of the neighbouring chateaux. Melanie would have gladly entered into the spirit of the occasion if only the nagging worry about Simon hadn't clawed its way back into her mind, though Brett had never mentioned him when he returned to the chateau.

By nine o'clock the long wooden trestles, covered with immaculate white tablecloths, were groaning under the weight of the buffet that Michel and his assistants had personally supervised. There were mouth-watering salads, fish and cold meats of every kind, quiches, flans, cheese soufflés, light as air, and creamy desserts, the like of which Melanie had never seen.

A trio played a well-known love song, and a voice behind her whispered, 'This tune's rather appropriate, don't you think?'

Brett whisked her on to the dance floor. They moved as one, her body fitting easily into his. He placed his arm around her waist, drawing her closer, and she closed her eyes as invisible sparks raced between them.

'Moments like this are why we live all the rest,' he murmured softly, and her breath was caught agonisingly in her throat.

Her head fell on his shoulder as they drifted, moved and danced around the floor. If only this could go on for ever, she thought to herself, as vibrant emotion consumed her. If only this would never end.

She had the distinct impression that someone was watching her, and as Brett excused himself to dance with one of the guests, she saw a man wearing black trousers and a fox's headdress standing on the edge of the dance floor. She couldn't see his face, but there was something about his stance that told her it was Simon.

'It's too hot in this thing,' he said, removing his headdress and throwing it on to the nearest table. 'Have you been avoiding me?'

'No,' Melanie replied. 'What's the point? I've nothing to say to you.'

'So you still refuse to cheat on my charming cousin?'

She rounded on him furiously.

'I've already told you. I want no part of your evil scheme.'

He seemed to be taking that in, then he said, 'I see. Well, there's always Dubois. I suppose as a last resort I could see him.'

He stopped there and it was impossible for her to guess what was in his mind, but warning bells rang in her head. Before she could ask what he meant, he excused himself, telling her there was someone he wanted to see. Even so, she couldn't rid herself of a feeling of unease.

I'm just over-reacting, she told herself. There's nothing to worry about. Nevertheless she wanted to be alone for a while and walked through the French doors and out into the cool, night air.

As she started to make her way across the terrace, she was stopped dead in her tracks as a hand reached out of the darkness and grabbed her. Shocked, she tried to regain her balance as she found herself falling backwards, and a small cry escaped from her throat.

'So you're our lovely hostess, are you?'

The voice was masculine and slurred by drink. She tried to run but a strong arm pinned her against the rough, stone wall. She could see the man more clearly now. He was tall, and from what she could discern in the darkness, a stranger to her.

'Please, let me go.'

Remembering Kate Usher's warning about unsavoury characters, she struggled with all her strength, but in spite of all her efforts, she stood no chance against him and his grip tightened.

'Not on your life,' he replied gruffly. 'You're supposed to look after the guests, aren't you? Isn't that part of your job? Well, I want you to look after me. Now stop struggling and give me a kiss.'

Desperate by now, Melanie moved her head from side to side, as he clutched her to him in a vain attempt to kiss her.

'Let me go!' she spat out. 'You're drunk and you're hurting me. You'll be sorry about this when you sober up. Do you want me to raise the alarm? Is that what you want?'

'I don't give a damn what you do,' he insisted, 'as long as you're nice to me.

Now you're going to be nice to me, aren't you?'

He staggered about on the darkened terrace, dragging her with him. Terrified by now, she would have welcomed some help, but felt she should deal with the situation herself. Surely if she kept her head, he would come to his senses and leave her alone.

'Come on now, stop struggling, kiss me!'

The man tottered drunkenly, leaning against her for support, trying to kiss her bare shoulder, covering her mouth with his hand. She was too scared by now to try and scream, even if she'd been able to. But somehow she managed to gather her wits together and she kicked him hard in the groin. He released her, recoiling with a cry of pain.

And now at last she saw someone, a man, walking across the terrace, and with profound relief she saw it was Brett. In an instant he realised what was going on. He caught the man, held him at arm's length and punched him hard on the jaw. Then rushing over to where Melanie stood, trembling, he took off his white tuxedo and placed it around her shoulders, speaking softly all the while, gaining her confidence, comforting her.

'Melanie, are you all right? That fellow obviously couldn't hold his drink. I wouldn't have had this happen for the world.'

'I'm all right, I'm all right, really,' she gasped. 'He was such a big man and I was so scared. Your mother warned me about people like that. But I never thought that here I'd be in danger.'

'Yes, even here,' Brett said softly. 'But he won't dare to show his face here again. He's just about managed to stagger off to his car. His chauffeur will have driven him away by now. Do you want to go to your room for a while?'

'No, I'd rather come back with you and join the guests.'

Melanie managed a faint smile.

'I've looked forward to this evening for so long.'

Brett took her hand and they walked over to where the drinks were being served.

'The wine's really going down,' he said, 'much faster than I thought. I'd better check with Pierre.'

He turned to talk to one of the barmen who was busily opening a bottle of muscadet.

'What do you think, Pierre?'

Pierre counted the bottles and shook his head.

'I regret, monsieur, but I doubt if we'll have enough left to last the evening.'

'I'm sure you're right.'

Brett checked the bottles himself.

'Tell me how many you think you'll need and I'll get Dubois to fetch them from the cellar.'

'Yes, of course, monsieur. Anton! Jacques!'

The barmen started to read the labels so they could list what was required.

'By the way, where is Dubois?' Brett enquired. 'I haven't seen him for quite a while. He loves a social occasion and it's most unlike him not to mingle with the guests. Do you think you could find him, Melanie? That is, if you feel up to it.'

'Yes, of course. I'll go and look for him.'

She could see there were several bottles left, so she didn't hurry. He was probably in the kitchen checking on the food supply. But when she saw he wasn't there, she searched the hall, the diningrooms, the terraces, but he was nowhere to be found. And now she thought about it, neither was Simon!

Suppose he'd found Jacques? Suppose Jacques had refused to give him the key? Would Simon still try to go ahead with his plan? Whatever had happened, Melanie didn't want to alarm Brett. After all, there was probably nothing wrong. She was just imagining things.

'I'm sorry, but I can't find Jacques

anywhere,' she said to Brett, in as calm a voice as she could muster. 'Perhaps he isn't feeling very well.'

'He looked perfectly well when I last saw him, about half an hour ago,' Brett said. 'Well, I can't leave it any longer. The wine's nearly run out. I'll just have to go to the wine cellar myself.'

He consulted his list.

'Anton, give me ten minutes to sort this lot out, then follow me down to the cellar and we'll bring up the bottles together.'

Melanie didn't wait to hear any more. She ran out of the chateau, across the terraces and down the flight of stone steps leading to the wine cellar. A terrible suspicion had formed in her mind. Had Simon somehow forced Jacques to hand over the key? Had he used brute force? He seemed desperate enough for anything, but was he desperate enough for that?

Her heart was pounding in her ears when she reached the cellar. Just as she'd suspected, the door was ajar and the lights were on. She ran inside, past the racks of country wines, the vintage wines, the champagnes. She didn't stop running until she came to that section of the cellar that housed the priceless wines.

It was then she saw Simon reading the label on one of the bottles, replacing that bottle in the rack and taking out another. He was holding a bottle in his hand when he looked up and saw her racing towards him.

'Simon, for goodness' sake,' she cried, 'how did you get the key?'

Simon didn't reply. He merely went on with what he was doing, appearing quite unconcerned.

'Simon, get out of here quickly,' she cried, her patience almost at an end. 'The wine's running out. We couldn't find Jacques, so Brett's coming down for the wine himself. He'll be here any second. Forget about the wine. Get out of here!'

At last she appeared to have got through to him. Snatching the nearest bottle from the rack, he grabbed her arm and pushed her in the direction of the door.

'Thanks, Melanie,' he said waving the bottle, 'but having come this far I've no intention of leaving this behind.'

Melanie hurried along, matching him stride for stride, all the time bombarding him with questions.

'Where's Jacques? No-one can find him. Has it anything to do with you?'

Simon remained unperturbed.

'Don't worry yourself about him. I knew he wouldn't give me the key. Stupid fool — he only got what he deserved.'

He broke off, his face paralysed with fear as he saw Brett coming down the steps towards them. Without a moment's hesitation he grabbed Melanie, and she found herself being clasped in a close embrace.

'Sorry,' Simon murmured, so only she could hear, and before she could put up any resistance, his mouth came down on hers.

Brett stopped a few feet away from them.

'I'm sorry to intrude on this tender scene,' he said, snatching the bottle from Simon. 'I'll take that if you don't mind. And the key as well. You're not getting away with it!'

Simon recoiled, backing away as Brett rounded on him furiously.

'Who gave you the key? Dubois? I hardly think so. You stole it from him, didn't you?'

He grabbed Simon by the throat while Melanie stood by helplessly.

'Where's Dubois? What have you done to him? Take me to him immediately, do you hear? Tell me what you've done with him or by God, I'll shake it out of you.'

'All right, old man, all right.'

Simon tried to regain some vestige of composure.

'Your precious Jacques is perfectly all right. A bit shaken perhaps, but otherwise OK.'

'Tell me where he is, or I'll . . . '

'What? Inform the police? I certainly wouldn't advise that with my record.'

Brett made as if to grab him again as Simon went on.

'All right, we'll make a deal. I'll tell you where he is, but only if you give me your word you'll let me go. And no police, mind. I'll go, old man, I'll go, and I'll never darken your door again.'

'All right, you have my word. I don't give a damn about you, but I am concerned about Dubois. Where is he?'

'He's in one of the outbuildings, you know, the one on the far left that hasn't been used for years.'

He grinned in a condescending way.

'Nobody would dream of looking for him there. I didn't hurt him, honest. I intended to let him go as soon as I'd got the wine.'

'Get out of my sight,' Brett told him brusquely. 'I must go to him at once. And as for you,' he said, turning to Melanie who had stood there listening to it all, 'I want words with you. And though I hate to spoil a good party, I'd prefer it if you didn't return to my guests. Go straight to my study and wait for me there. Is that clear?'

'It's not her fault,' Simon blurted out, as Melanie merely nodded.

Too shattered to speak, she watched Brett stride away in the direction of the outbuildings. Her distress was tearing her apart. After what he'd just seen, nothing she could say would make him believe she wasn't Simon's accomplice.

She walked over to his study in sombre mood, and when he walked into the room, her concern was all for Jacques.

'Well, did you find him?'

Brett nodded brusquely, refusing to be drawn.

'Is he all right?'

He looked at her coldly.

'Yes, no thanks to you and my cousin. Perhaps you'd care to explain your part in this little affair.'

Melanie gripped her hands together, fighting desperately for control.

'I know it looked bad, as if I were in

league with Simon, but if you'll just let me explain . . . '

She broke off, biting her lower lip, trying to put it into words he would understand.

'Going down to the wine cellar was the last thing I wanted to do,' she began again.

'So he carried you down there, did he? Is that what you expect me to believe?'

'Don't be absurd. He told me earlier he was desperate for cash. He wanted a bottle of your wine so he could sell it to finance a deal.'

'What kind of deal?'

'I don't know. With some local winery, I suppose. He didn't tell me the details.'

'So my silver-tongued cousin persuaded you to steal.'

'No, not steal. He asked me to try and borrow the key to the wine cellar. Of course, I refused.'

'Just what was it that he said?'

'He said he was desperate, that he'd

told you about this business deal but you'd refused to help him. He said that you'd swindled him out of a fortune and if I could just get the key . . . '

'You'd be as guilty as him. Taking the key was tantamount to stealing the wine. Surely you realised that?'

'Yes, I did. Of course, I did. And I told him I'd have no part in it. But he still wanted the wine. He said if I refused to help him get the key, he'd have to get it some other way.'

'So you knew he'd stolen the key from Dubois?'

'Of course I didn't know. It was pure supposition on my part. But when Jacques couldn't be found, some instinct or other made me think of Simon and connect him with what might have happened.'

'How clever of you. And just what did you think Simon had done?'

'I don't know. I thought perhaps he'd tricked Jacques into giving him the key. Or . . . '

'Taken it by force? That's more like

it, isn't it? Don't you realise yet what a scoundrel he is?'

'Yes, of course I do. But he sounded so sincere. He said that if the deal was to go through, he had to raise some cash at any price.'

'And you didn't think the price too high? What other guilty secrets are you keeping from me, I wonder.'

'I haven't any secrets. I'm not guilty. I swear it. Not guilty of betraying you as you seem to think. I'm so sorry about it all. And I'm so worried about Jacques. Please say that he's all right.'

'It's a wonder he came out of it as well as he did. Simon wouldn't have thought twice about beating him about the head if he couldn't get his own way. He's a ruthless swine. I don't know how you could bear him near you.'

'I couldn't. I didn't. There was nothing I could do.'

'He kissed you!'

'He's stronger than I am. He'd grabbed me before I could stop him. How was I to know what he was going to do? You don't believe me, do you? I've told you I couldn't stop him. Aren't you convinced yet?'

His face was granite hard.

'I'm far from convinced. From where I stood you seemed to be co-operating admirably.'

She swallowed hard and looked at him, her eyes blazing defiance.

'For goodness' sake, Brett!'

'Don't play the innocent with me. You cheated me. You accepted my help, my hospitality, my home, and you cheated me.'

Walking over to the door he flung it open, before turning round to face her.

'I'm terminating your employment as of now. You will leave the chateau as soon as it's daylight. Now go, and pack your things!'

8

Turning abruptly on his heel he strode away, leaving her shocked and bewildered by his uncompromising stance. She was shaking with anger, with fear, afraid to lash out at him again, and unsure she could hold on to her self control.

No matter what she did, no matter what she said, he had no intention of believing her.

Through the open door she could hear the strains of music, and see brilliant flashes of light. The fireworks display had begun. She watched as rockets and starburst wheels swirled up into the darkness, leaving trails of fire in their wake. In any other circumstances she would have joined in the revels, but tonight Brett had verbally abused her, and despite what his mother had said, he'd made it obvious he didn't love her.

She'd have given anything to turn back the clock.

Now that she'd been told to leave, she'd lose everything. And worst of all, she'd lost the man she loved. When he'd walked away from her, he'd taken with him all her dreams, her desires, her hopes for the future, and the pain she felt was one continuous ribbon of fire.

Walking back to her rooms, the sounds of revelling drifted back to her from the terraces. Some of the guests were leaving and she could hear a crescendo of voices, laughter, car doors slamming, joyous farewells.

And her own farewell wasn't so far away.

He'd told her to leave at daybreak, but what was the point of waiting until then? If she wanted to keep her sanity and self respect she had to go now, immediately. She ran through the hall, up to her suite, packed an overnight bag and picked up her car keys. She'd drive to Chinon and stay there for the night while she thought things through.

She crept downstairs, not wanting to be seen by anyone, not wanting to have to explain why she was leaving. Running to the stables where the cars were parked, she found the small, blue car Brett had told her was for her own exclusive use, and throwing her bag on to the back seat, she started the engine.

Blinded by sobs, she could hardly see through the windscreen as she drove down the drive, and she dabbed at her eyes with the back of her hand.

She couldn't remember which way to go. She'd been so busy with work, that she hadn't had time to explore the local region, and anyway places looked different in the dark. She knew Chinon was the nearest town.

When she got to the top of the avenue of limes, she turned left and drove on, castigating herself, hating Brett, determined never to return. But she seemed to be driving in the wrong direction, and she hadn't thought to take a map.

After a while some instinct told her to check the fuel gauge, and her worst fears were realised — it registered empty! She had to get out of the car.

She paced up and down in a kind of blank despair. Black as a raven's wing, the night closed in around her. She climbed back into the driver's seat, her fingers drumming impatiently on the steering wheel. There was no point in trying to start the engine. What was she going to do?

Then she saw the headlights of a car and relief flooded through her as Brett's Land-Rover swerved to a halt.

'What the devil do you think you're doing?' he shouted, his face etched with concern. 'The entire staff's been searching for you. I didn't think of checking on your car. I didn't think you'd be fool enough to drive away at this time of night on your own. What got into you? And you can leave that thing here,' he went on, indicating her small car.

'But . . . '

'Don't argue,' he said with dangerous softness. 'Get into the car. You're coming back with me.'

He settled her into the passenger seat of the Land-Rover and slammed the door.

'You still think I want you to leave?' he enquired, as he started up the engine. 'I never wanted you to leave. Quite apart from Simon's futile attempt to steal the wine, it was my own stupid jealousy at seeing him kiss you that sent me into orbit the way it did.'

'But I didn't have anything to do with Simon.'

'I know you didn't. You acted in good faith, and my mother's just given me a piece of her mind for acting like a fool.'

Melanie could tell his thoughts were in turmoil, and she crouched in the passenger seat, hardly daring to look at him.

'Are you all right?' he went on. 'You must have been scared to death, out on your own at this time of night when you didn't know the road.'

'And the fuel had run out,' she explained, a nervous pulse beating forcefully in her throat. 'I really didn't know what to do. If you hadn't come . . . '

'But I did, and I'm here and I'm never going to let you out of my sight again.'

He squeezed her arm.

'I've been a fool,' he said. 'I should have realised there was nothing between you and Simon, but because of my insane jealousy I was shocked and angry. How can I begin to apologise for the way I behaved? It was stupid and unforgivable. I couldn't bear it if you left me,' he went on. 'Please say you'll stay.'

The tremor in his voice and the expression in his eyes hit her like a bolt of lightning. She knew in her heart he honestly meant what he'd said. But that didn't stop her from feeling hurt and abused.

'Look at me, Melanie. Don't you

realise yet how much I regret all the things I said?'

Looking at him, seeing the expression in his eyes, hearing his voice, she knew she couldn't stay angry with him for long.

'Yes, of course I do, Brett,' she said softly, 'and it would break my heart to leave.'

★ ★ ★

Stopping the car at the main door of the chateau, he ran round to help her out of the passenger seat. All the guests had gone, but Kate Usher was waiting for them just inside the great hall. As soon as she saw Melanie, she gave a little cry.

'Melanie, thank goodness you're safe. I've been so worried about you. Well, we all have. Jacques,' she went on, as the major domo came rushing forward to add his welcome, 'the girl's exhausted. Bring her some brandy and be quick about it. Look at her, she's trembling. She's obviously been through a frightful ordeal and it's all your fault, Brett. You don't deserve her, really you don't. I hope you're going to make it up to her.'

'Don't worry, Mother, I intend to,' Brett declared, 'if it takes me the rest to my life.'

The rest of his life? Melanie could hardly believe her ears. Whatever did he mean by that? He'd never said he loved her, not once. And he never would.

She gave a little sigh. The events of the night might have brought her anguish and pain, but loving someone who did not love you was the cruellest form of suffering.

The brandy scorched the back of her throat. She still felt dizzy and disorientated after her ordeal.

'And don't think I only blame Brett,' Kate Usher went on.

She took Melanie's hand in hers.

'I, myself, feel partly to blame. What a wretch Simon turned out to be. If he hadn't tried to blackmail Brett the way he did, none of this would ever have happened. And he tried to use you as well. He'll never have the audacity to come here again.'

Melanie finished her drink.

'I think I'll go up to my room now, if you don't mind,' she said in a voice that still shook slightly.

'Yes, of course.'

Brett was instantly on his feet.

'No, please. I'd rather go alone. Thank you all for worrying about me,' she went on, managing a smile. 'I'm sure I'll feel better in the morning. A good night's sleep works wonders, doesn't it?'

As she climbed the stairs she saw Jacques Dubois waiting outside her room.

'I just wanted to make sure you were all right, mademoiselle,' he said, 'before I retired for the night.'

'Jacques, how kind of you,' Melanie replied. 'I've been so worried about what happened to you.'

He shrugged.

'Ah, you are not to worry your pretty head about me,' he said. 'What happened was not your fault. Monsieur Simon, he ask me for the key to the special wines. Well, of course, I could not allow him to have it. No-one can have the key without asking Monsieur Brett. It is a matter of loyalty, you see.'

Melanie's eyes scanned his face.

'What did he do to you, Jacques? Did he hurt you? He said he'd left you in one of the outhouses.'

She decided to tell him what had transpired.

'You see, Simon wanted me to help him, too, but naturally I refused. He knew only you and Brett had a key, and there was no likelihood of Brett giving it to him.'

'Ah, no, of course not. Monsieur Brett would never give him the key. Monsieur Simon has been to the chateau before, mademoiselle. He pretends he has come to see his aunt, but that is not the truth. It is for money he comes.'

'But, Jacques, what did Simon do to you to get the key? Did he hurt you?'

'A few bruises, perhaps. He is younger than me and more strong. But Monsieur Brett send him away. A good riddance, too, I think!' Jacques added with a wry grin.

'So he's already left the chateau?'

'He left immediately, mademoiselle. Now are you sure there's nothing further I can do?'

'Nothing, thank you, Jacques. I've been through a lot tonight one way or another. Let's hope tomorrow brings with it some semblance of normality.'

Melanie gave Jacques a gentle hug which the older man seemed to appreciate, before she headed into her room.

She undressed in a feeling of being in a dream, but gradually she began to relax, and after a warm soak in a luxurious, foaming bath, she relaxed into a sleep which was full of dreams of the man who had captured her heart in so short a time.

9

Next morning Melanie awoke to the sound of tinkling china and the smell of freshly-brewed coffee. Ann-Marie, one of the maids at the chateau, was standing beside her bed.

'Monsieur Brett gave strict instructions not to disturb you before noon, mademoiselle. I have brought your usual breakfast, but if you would prefer something more substantial, Michel will prepare something.'

'No,' Melanie said, stretching her arms above her head. 'Thank you, Ann-Marie, that will be fine. Phew, I must have slept for hours.'

'Ten hours to be exact,' Ann-Marie replied with a smile. 'You were exhausted, mademoiselle, and we were all so worried about you, especially Monsieur Brett. Michel said to tell you he is preparing something extra special for dinner tonight, for you and Monsieur Brett, that is.'

Propped up against the pillows, Melanie bit into Michel's deliciously-light croissant, the events of the previous night spinning around in her head. So much had happened during the last twenty-four hours. Some things she wanted to remember, others she wanted to forget. That unpleasant encounter on the terrace, for instance, and her later confrontation with Brett. But she must consign them to the back of her mind. Brett had been as anxious to make amends as she was to forgive. She loved him and she knew she would go on loving him for the rest of her life.

After she'd showered and dressed, she walked out on to the terrace. She was lost in her reminiscences of when she'd first arrived at the chateau, when she heard a sound behind her and a strong pair of arms encircled her waist.

'Melanie, we have to talk,' Brett said. 'There's so much left unsaid, and my behaviour last night was quite out of order. Can you ever forgive those dreadful things I said?'

He turned her round to face him and slowly, very slowly, he bent his head and kissed her, revelling in her response, as her whole body thrilled to a quivering frisson of sensation. Gently releasing her he smiled.

'I think I've got my answer. Marry me, Melanie. I can't imagine life without you.'

Her previous doubts about his feelings for her disappeared as if by magic.

'You mean you do love me?'

For answer he smiled and cradled her in his arms.

'I think I've loved you from the first moment we met, that first day at Squirrels' Chase. I saw you and took a deep breath. When I breathed out, I was in love.'

'And I love you.'

Melanie threw her arms around his neck.

'Do you really want me to marry you?'

'Of course I do. I've told you I love you.'

'I know. But say it again. I want to get used to hearing how it sounds.'

He told her again.

'Well?' he queried with a smile, 'how does it sound?'

'It sounds wonderful. My only regret is that Father isn't here to see how happy I am. I still can't forgive myself for not realising how much trouble he was in.'

Brett smoothed her long, blonde hair.

'He didn't want you to know. He cared for you too much to burden you with the failure of his business ventures. And he had too much pride. The stress of it all was too much for him to bear.'

He paused to make sure Melanie wasn't too upset by what he'd told her, before he continued.

'On a lighter note, Michel is preparing something special for supper tonight. And with all the guests gone, it will be just you and me. Forgive me for neglecting you, now, though, but I need to plod on with some routine work for the rest of the day. I'm afraid it can't wait. It will be difficult though. Now that we're going to be married, I'll have the devil's own job trying to concentrate.'

He laughed.

Later, they ate out on the terrace, and toasted each other in champagne.

'Now,' he said, 'before we get too carried away, I'm anxious to make some wedding plans, if you feel up to it.'

'Yes, I feel fine,' she replied as he replenished her glass. 'What do you have in mind?'

'Give me a moment, I'm thinking. If we have a big wedding we'll have to invite all our friends, my relations, my business associates and . . . '

He mused for a moment.

'Melanie, my love, it's entirely up to you, but I think I'd prefer a quiet, simple ceremony in the old-fashioned church in Richelieu. You haven't seen it yet, but I can soon take you there. We could go on our honeymoon, abroad if you like. And when we come back we could have a big celebration at the chateau.'

He looked at her rather uncertainly.

'Of course, it's just an idea.'

'Oh, Brett, it's a wonderful idea. I can't think of anything I'd like better.'

Lifting her off her feet, he swung her high in the air in delight.

'And as for your wedding gift, well, that's to be a surprise. And don't try and wheedle it out of me, because I've no intention of telling you what it is!'

The following day they visited the tiny sixteenth-century church in Richelieu. Melanie was charmed by it. Monsieur le Curé was delighted to see them.

'So this is your bride-to-be,' he said, kissing Melanie on both cheeks in the French fashion. 'I'd given up on Brett finding a wife,' he went on. 'In the past, whenever I questioned him about it, he said he couldn't marry because he'd never been in love.'

Brett grinned.

'That's true, I hadn't, until I met this lovely girl.'

'Yes, she is lovely, isn't she?' the priest replied, holding Melanie out at arms' length. 'All I need to know is that you love him, too.'

'Yes, oh, yes,' Melanie said, smiling. 'I'll never love anyone else.'

'Better and better,' the priest said, clapping his hands. 'But first things first. Let me consult my diary so we can fix a date for the wedding. I can manage it in two weeks time,' he said, entering their names. 'Where are you going for your honeymoon?'

'We haven't decided yet,' Brett said. 'Everything's happened so quickly. We hope we can count on you to come to the chateau after the ceremony,' he went on. 'We'd like you to join us in drinking a toast to our future happiness.'

'In your best champagne, of course,' the priest replied. 'How can I resist?'

Following their simple but very moving marriage ceremony, a champagne reception was held at the chateau for a few close friends, and Monsieur le Curé surprised everyone by showing how he could open a bottle of champagne with a knife!

Michel had refused to discuss the buffet. When Melanie asked him what he had planned, he just put a finger to the side of his nose and said, 'Wait!'

'I've a feeling it will involve oysters and wine,' Melanie told Brett, 'but we'll just have to wait and see.'

When all the guests had gone and they were finally alone, they sat on the terrace mulling over the events of the day.

'I tell you what,' Brett said, enfolding Melanie in his arms, 'let's not bother going to any of those places we discussed at the reception. I've got a better idea. Trust me!'

All the way to Cherbourg, even

during the Channel crossing, Melanie tried to find out where they were going.

'Oh, come on,' she implored Brett, 'tell me what you've got in mind. The suspense is killing me.'

'No.' He laughed. 'It will spoil the surprise. I hatched this little plan some time ago, and I'm not going to have it ruined now. Be patient, my love, for a little while longer. Now, let's go up on deck and enjoy the crossing. The water's as calm as a mill pond today.'

They drove off the ferry on a mellow, September afternoon. The English countryside was a palette of autumn tints, red, gold, amber and brown, and the fallen leaves were heaped into piles at the side of the road.

As Brett took an all-too-familiar route, Melanie suddenly guessed where he was taking her, but decided to humour him. When they reached the village pub, Brett must have realised she knew they were heading for Squirrels' Chase, but he decided to keep up the pretence for a little while longer.

'I want you to close your eyes,' he said, 'and don't open them until I tell you.'

Melanie wondered what he was up to, but did as she was told.

'All right, you can open them now,' he said, as they approached the gates leading to the estate.

She did so, and looked round, her eyes wide in amazement, as Brett parked outside the front entrance and helped her out of the passenger seat.

'When we left the chateau, I didn't think for one moment that we'd be coming here,' she said, with a touch of sadness in her voice, 'but I think I understand why you brought me. You knew I couldn't bear to see the old house go to rack and ruin. You also knew it would please me to see it restored, even if it does belong to Leisuresearch.'

Scaffolding and workmen were everywhere. In the months since she'd been away, some of the renovation work had already been completed, but there was still some work to be done.

'They've certainly got on with it, haven't they?' she said, impressed. 'What a difference a few months have made. Are the caretakers still here?'

'Yes, they're expecting us. I thought tea in the library would be welcome after that long drive.'

Following Melanie's gaze, he examined the renovation of the stonework.

'The house looks better already,' he said, 'and the gardens have been tidied up as you can see. Oh, and a new central heating system's been installed, so you won't be cold tonight.'

She laughed. Cold? She knew she would never be cold again, or frightened, or alone.

Taking her arm, Brett led her into the library, and opening a safe in the wall, he withdrew a large, brown package and handed it to her.

'You've waited a long time, but here's your wedding gift,' he said.

'But what about these?' she queried, touching the sapphire earrings Brett had given her when they became engaged.

Brett laughed.

'Those were only to treat you,' he said. 'Look in that envelope. That is your real wedding gift.'

With trembling fingers, Melanie opened the package and withdrew what appeared to be a legal document made out in the names of Mr and Mrs Brett Usher.

'What on earth!' she exclaimed.

But when she examined it more closely she realised it was the deeds to Squirrels' Chase.

'You've bought it for us?' she queried. 'From Leisuresearch? Oh, darling, never in my wildest dreams would I have thought it would ever be mine again.'

'Everyone has dreams,' he said, putting his arm around her waist. 'And my rôle in life is to make yours come true.'

In answer she gave him a long, passionate kiss.

'I want Squirrels' Chase to be our real home,' she said. 'But when you go away on business, I want to go with you. That is until we have children,' she added, with a twinkle in her eyes.

'But first we need some time to be together. There's still so much we have to learn about each other.'

Brett smiled and turned to face her.

'And we will learn. I say, I don't know about you, but I'm hungry.'

He glanced at his watch.

'Oh, good, tea will be arriving any minute. I expect they thought they'd leave us alone for a while. And as for dinner tonight, I've already arranged it.'

'That's brilliant,' Melanie replied. 'We're lucky some parts of the house are habitable. What could compare with having dinner in our own home? And on the subject of dinner, what have you done with the wine?'

'It's in the boot,' Brett replied,

amused. 'Surely you didn't think I'd forget it!'

Moving towards the window he beckoned to her to join him.

'Come quickly and look at these,' he said. 'Now we really know we're home.'

Looking out, Melanie saw three grey squirrels chasing each other across the lawn.

'Home will always be where you are, my darling,' she whispered softly. 'I love you.'

THE END

We do hope that you have enjoyed reading this large print book.

Did you know that all of our titles are available for purchase?

We publish a wide range of high quality large print books including:
Romances, Mysteries, Classics
General Fiction
Non Fiction and Westerns

Special interest titles available in large print are:
The Little Oxford Dictionary
Music Book, Song Book
Hymn Book, Service Book

Also available from us courtesy of Oxford University Press:
Young Readers' Dictionary
(large print edition)
Young Readers' Thesaurus
(large print edition)

For further information or a free brochure, please contact us at:
Ulverscroft Large Print Books Ltd.,
The Green, Bradgate Road, Anstey,
Leicester, LE7 7FU, England.
Tel: (00 44) **0116 236 4325**
Fax: (00 44) **0116 234 0205**

THREE TALL TAMARISKS

Christine Briscomb

Joanna Baxter flies from Sydney to run her parents' small farm in the Adelaide Hills while they recover from a road accident. But after crossing swords with Riley Kemp, life is anything but uneventful. Gradually she discovers that Riley's passionate nature and quirky sense of humour are capturing her emotions, but a magical day spent with him on the coast comes to an abrupt end when the elegant Greta intervenes. Did Riley love Greta after all?

SUMMER IN
HANOVER SQUARE

Charlotte Grey

The impoverished Margaret Lambart is suddenly flung into all the glitter of the Season in Regency London. Suspected by her godmother's nephew, the influential Marquis St. George, of being merely a common adventuress, she has, nevertheless, a brilliant success, and attracts the attentions of the young Duke of Oxford. However, when the Marquis discovers that Margaret is far from wanting a husband he finds he has to revise his estimate of her true worth.

Demanding the Impossible?